RICHARD BYRNE BSC(HONS)

MAYA ACCORD

novum pro

© 2022 novum publishing

ISBN 978-3-99131-314-4
Editing: Hugo Chandler, BA
Cover photos: Mooikunst, Thitiwat Dutsadeewirot, Kucheruk, Hootie2710 | Dreamstime.com
Cover design, layout & typesetting: novum publishing
Internal illustrations, Author's photo: Richard Byrne BSc(Hons)

www.novum-publishing.co.uk

FORWARD

Being a Christian, to the author, means having a working faith that is beyond question. The author wrote two books 'Dig the Dry Zone 1914' and 'Dig the Zone of Freedom 1916' but both books had no social impact. Writing about musical hymns and being a good person is not all that is needed to repair social ills. In the literary world of today it is not about writing a book with a brilliant story, or even getting it all over the internet that makes it successful.

The author's working faith methodology has been changed to accomplish a feasible target. Readers require a link to themselves. So, to spice things up, by using sex as a comprehensive social issue, alongside politics, religion, education, gender and ethnicity, that involves everyone, the author has created a musical play. Using an educational story and making a musical template for teenagers amplifies mankind's belief in life creating a musical dream of what religion is all about.

There is a large majority of working-class teenagers who are employed but are still living in social deprivation. When teenagers see the church and the Bible, it goes over their heads, simply because it fails to give them any immediate social benefit. The Maya Accord has been put together in their language with current real-life material events that teenagers can relate to. Thus, it gives them an immediate physical benefit that works. It has a positive effect on their understanding that they can make something satisfying in their lives come true giving them a more enjoyable future.

The true value of religion today is sometimes overlooked by differing interpretations of what is socially right in society. Angel Michael and Angel Gabriel were not born as angels, but rather grew into angels. Mary in her virginity became the Virgin Mary when she became pregnant. Even Jesus Christ's first miracle, turned several barrels of water into wine at a wedding reception – a dream come true for many alcoholics! Saint Paul who wrote several letters in the New Testament, in his earlier years known as Saul, captured and had many Christians put to death. Churches today profess that sex outside of marriage is a sin. Many members of the church profess not to be sinners. Today, couples of the same sex can legally be married in church. The author was at a Sunday morning church service and talking to members of the congregation explained to them that Mary, as in the Bible, was not married to Joseph when she gave birth to Jesus Christ. They replied that I was mistaken. Joseph and Mary were husband and wife before she gave birth. The author replied – 'are you trying to tell me that Mary was not a virgin?'

INTRODUCTION

The author would like to make clear from the outset that the objective of the Maya Accord is to help teenagers, who have a growing drug need that they don't want to continue with, by providing them with an alternative to methadone.

The Maya Accord is not in itself replacing an addiction with another addiction but is more a case of replacing a bad taste with a feeling of euphoria or 'buzz!' A number of university students to get a buzz out of life, try drugs; these are mostly middle class teenagers who in time grow out of their wanting to walk on the wild side. It is the working class teenagers who are trying to get the best buzz they can out of life making cheap drug- related deaths rampant throughout the world.
For those teenagers who want to stop taking drugs the Maya Accord methodology helps to tackle their drug affliction before it becomes an addiction.

The Maya Accord story line is that the Virgin Mary, Adam and Eve, Angels Michael and Gabriel find themselves on an ark captained by Maya the Goddess of Recovery. Dropping from the sky as a rainbow, they return to planet Earth with the intention of saving the world.
As a musical play, the Maya Accord has been performed by the Maya Ark Youth Accord drama group in a recording studio in Brighton.

CAST

MAYA – is a God (Mr Speaker)
pretending to be a Goddess
MARY – Virgin Volunteer
ADAM – Choir Master
EVE – Volunteer
MICHAEL – Angel
GABRIEL – Angel
TEENAGE CHOIR

MUSIC

ACT ONE

SET – ARK CHAPEL BELOW DECK
NAVE

*** MUSIC – APPENDIX 2

LED SCREEN

City of hope hear our plea	Come gracious Lord
Give us your word	Sing heavenly King
Help us see	Light and Love
Teach us true we are so blue	O set us free
Give us your grace in this place	With a true love be

ENTER PROCESSION SINGING TEENAGE CHOIR waving BANNERS and FLAGS; EVE and MARY as graduates each wearing CAP and GOWN, with ANGELS MICHAEL and GABRIEL as NUNS wearing HABITS following behind.
TEENAGE CHOIR splits into two and they go either side of ADAM and MAYA on the CHANCEL, to their respective CHOIR PEWS.
ADAM stands between TWO SETS of CHOIR PEWS.
MAYA GODDESS OF RECOVERY SITS before an ALTAR with ANGELS MICHAEL and GABRIEL STANDING on either side.
EVE and MARY, HOLDING HANDS, STAND BEFORE the CHANCEL.

MICHAEL   What does being a Christian mean?
GABRIEL   We both have a working faith that is be-
           yond question.
MARY   Be realistic! What is physically possible?

LED SCREEN.

ACT ONE
CROSS-PARTY TALK

BETWEEN CHOIR PEWS
ADAM   They call me Adam. I'm a choir master help-
           ing in this Ark of Life. When things are out
           of tune, who else is there to blame. My work-
           ing faith has not achieved a social solution.

BEFORE ALTAR.
MAYA   I am Maya the Goddess of Recovery. My
           civilization died a thousand years ago and left
           me as their Madam Deputy Speaker sailing
           this Ark around the universe. As a Goddess
           singing hymns in heaven is just not good
           enough. We must impact on society and
           solve social ill on this planet they call earth.
           I know everything, but what is KY?

BEFORE CHANCEL
EVE   There are some things in life that ladies don't
           talk about. They call me Eve. I tried it once
           with the Angels Michael and Gabriel but it
           didn't work out. I used to be an addict but

	since Mary and I have been here in this Ark I've dried out.
MARY	We're both graduates from Cambridge, but when she was an addict, I lived in a different world.

ANGELS GABRIEL and MICHAEL, DRESSED as NUNS, each holding a PILLOW move to the CHANCEL.

CHANCEL

GABRIEL	Who are we? Why do we as angels have to dress up as Nuns? (puts his hand on his hip).
MICHAEL	I'm the Angel Michael and you're the Angel Gabriel, but our work here on this Maya Ark cannot be done by Angels.
GABRIEL	I like the idea of both of us being sisters together.
MICHAEL	This will liven things up! My pillow is to represent the birth of a true way of life, whatever that might be.
GABRIEL	As Nuns we shall be symbolic of purity in earthly places. (puts his arm around MICHAEL's shoulders).
MICHAEL	To turn what is seen as bad into something good. Methodology you use is incorrect.
GABRIEL	We must all simply say the truth if we don't already. (pulls a fan from his habit and fans himself).
MICHAEL	I get embarrassed sometimes. Our cousin is the Angel Lucifer.
GABRIEL	We all like to get a good buzz out of life. We were asking sinful nations not to sin.
MICHAEL	It's a sexual buzz that makes a man a man. A boy meets a girl and she, after finding out

GABRIEL   she can't get any satisfaction, hangs him out to dry.

GABRIEL   Women are like that! A young man finds himself left on his own without a buzz, so he becomes prey to drug dealers. (shines a torch down the front of his habit).

MICHAEL   He gets a bigger buzz out of taking drugs.

GABRIEL   We are all searching for that bigger buzz! We must change things! Instead of Adam and Eve in the beginning let's change it so the birth of our saviour comes first.

MICHAEL   That's why I'm an Angel.

GABRIEL   There's only one buzz greater than ours. Then Adam and Eve could as twins be conceived in a stable.

ANGELS GABRIEL and MICHAEL stuff the PILLOWS they are holding up the front of their HABITS so they both LOOK PREGNANT.

GABRIEL   We must all learn from the mistakes we make.

MICHAEL   When you find satisfaction with a friend, keep it a secret. it lasts longer that way.

GABRIEL   Both of us must first go to hospital for a pregnancy test, just in case! (looks at himself in a hand- mirror).

MICHAEL   Some women pretend to be pregnant – then it actually happens.

GABRIEL   Sisters of the world! We shall give birth to our living truth. We could solve community problems before they start by casting politics, gender issues, ethnicity and unwanted pregnancy to the wind.

MICHAEL   I'm getting excited! If anyone asks I'll tell
               them not to eat so much barley bread or
               they'll look like me.

ALTAR
MAYA   I am Madam Speaker of the Ark. There are
               things in life, such as a maya accord, that
               nobody seems to understand. Show me the
               minutes of this cross-party talk?

BETWEEN CHOIR PEWS
ADAM   But Madam Speaker you're not supposed to
               be here yet! The Angels Michael and Gabriel
               are still putting the minutes on KY together.

ALTAR
MAYA   It doesn't matter where you are! This Ark
               is a Parliament of Heaven. It shall solve so-
               cial deprivation on the planet earth. Church
               life and a new bible that I shall create will
               no longer fly over the heads of teenagers.

BETWEEN CHOIR PEWS
ADAM   Laws of truth and righteousness are often
               impossible to follow. We call these minutes
               forward for consideration.

ALTAR
MAYA   I blame all middle-class realms of debauch-
               ery and politics on my brother Lucifer. I
               shall be down to earth in all things so he as
               a satanic devil becomes confused with the
               power Alpha and Omega.

BETWEEN CHOIR PEWS
ADAM   I remember Madam Speaker! I overheard
              the Cambridge graduate volunteers Eve and
              Mary telling newspaper reporters you rep-
              resent a complexity.

ALTAR
MAYA   As Madam Speaker of the Ark I should like
              all members to know I'm not a middle-class
              everyday trombonist in drag with nothing
              better to do.

BETWEEN CHOIR PEWS
ADAM   But why Madam Speaker do we need two
              volunteers Eve and Mary in this saga?

ALTAR
MAYA   They may be just bell ringers at this mo-
              ment, but Eve and Mary are to shape the
              destiny of mankind.

EVE and MARY in graduate caps and gowns, HOLDING
HANDS, move to the front of the CHANCEL

CHANCEL
EVE   No peace for those who profess to be clever.
              Our Maya Accord is to be a working faith
              that all teenagers can relate to.
MARY   Its social benefits will be immediate! Gideon
              New Testament 2009 Page 699.
EVE   1 Corinthians argues it is written 'I shall
              destroy the wisdom of the wise. The intel-
              ligence of the intelligent I shall frustrate.'
              All women need KY!

MARY   I shall open their eyes! Those that cannot
                get satisfaction will have a more enjoyable
                future. Let us sing!

CHOIR PEWS

*** MUSIC — APPENDIX 3

LED SCREEN

Seek the throne of grace.
It's in every place.
When we live in prayer
Truth is present everywhere.
TEENAGE CHOIR SINGS with ADAM CONDUCTING.

EVE and MARY, HOLDING HANDS, move before the
CHANCEL.

CHANCEL
ADAM moves to the FRONT of the CHANCEL.
ADAM   Does a congregation of young teenagers
                sometimes have difficulty singing in tune?

ALTAR
MAYA   Is the textbook way of doing things their con-
                ductor? Look at life from their point of view!

CHANCEL
ADAM   Do teenagers want us to sing out of tune? It
                is their right to make that choice.

ALTAR
MAYA   But the limit is when the seven heads of
               Lucifer appear, with ten horns, and seven
               crowns. Here in front of us now teenagers
               have the answer. They've just got to learn
               to do things in a different way.

CHANCEL
ADAM   When teenagers have recovered from their
               addictions they will go back to earth, look-
               ing for a narrow gate. Religion today has
               many different interpretations that give us
               a social position in life.

ALTAR
MAYA   What's wrong with that? My plans have been
               written to challenge the thoughts of others
               by making life for teenagers more liveable.

ADAM joins EVE and MARY BEFORE the CHANCEL

BEFORE CHANCEL
ADAM   It is the choices we implement that make us
               who we are.
EVE   It is written that love is the bread of life.
MARY   Then how come I hunger for satisfaction?
               Could it be that love only creates all the evil
               problems of life.
ADAM   But the answer is staring us in the face! We
               must open our eyes and see the truth.
EVE   Then what is love?
MARY   Love represents a girl and boy getting mar-
               ried and making babies.

| ADAM | Undertaking the repercussions of love caus-
es abuse in all its forms, poverty, unthinka-
ble crimes, and divorce. |

CONGREGATION
ANGELS MICHAEL and GABRIEL STAND

MICHAEL	That hospital triage nurse said she found it hard to believe due to us both being Nuns.
GABRIEL	We were not born angels. There's no point us trying to justify the cause. We've both been invaded.
MICHAEL	So, I told her it was posterity in disguise!

ANGELS MICHAEL and GABRIEL move to the CHANCEL

GABRIEL	We've got to go back tomorrow for a pos- itive or negative confirmation. What if its positive and we're both pregnant?
MICHAEL	I'm only pretending! How could it be?
GABRIEL	Who knows? Yours could have twins!

ALTAR

| MAYA | Order! I think heaven's first attempt send-
ing a saviour to save the world got it wrong.
Many questions are left unanswered. |

CHANCEL

| GABRIEL | We're in heaven's House of Commons to-
gether! If we're pregnant Madam Deputy
Speaker, are you the father or not? |
| MICHAEL | Could it be Madam Deputy Speaker that
you are using me to develop an answer? I
agree the Old Testament should have started |

with the birth of the Virgin Mary's son not
Adam and Eve.

GABRIEL   Could it be we are part of a solution?

ANGELS MICHAEL and GABRIEL, join the TEENAGE
CHOIR on either side in their respective DISPATCH BOX.

ALTAR
MAYA   Order! I agree the Old Testament is to be
               re-written. Prime Minister, Angel Michael
               is called to give a statement to the house.

DISPATCH BOX 1
MICHAEL   Madam Deputy Speaker! Nature is a fan-
               tastic thing! It makes this dodgy world go
               round. Saint Paul, previously known as Saul,
               started his career by having Christians put
               to death.

DESPATCH BOX 2
GABRIEL   As sisters of the cloth we're not meant to get
               pregnant. In heaven we sometimes make the
               wrong choices.

ALTAR
MAYA   Order! Will the Leader of the Opposition
               Angel Gabriel let the Prime Minister fin-
               ish his opening statement. Prime Minister!

DISPATCH BOX 1
MICHAEL   Madam Deputy Speaker! That's why our
               first saviour of mankind demonstrated and
               turned barrels of water into wine. He knew
               we had got it wrong.

CHANCEL
ADAM, EVE and MARY move to the FRONT of the
CHANCEL

EVE   If I believe in myself I shall never die.
MARY   Sounds a bit like quantum physics,
               unbelievable!
ADAM   We must eat our own flesh and drink our
               own blood.
EVE   I agree!
MARY   Me too!

ALTAR
MAYA   Order! Leader of the Opposition!

DISPATCH BOX 2
GABRIEL   Madam Deputy Speaker! Hospital doctors
               have just sent us a text. Thank the Lord!
               Angel Michael is not pregnant.

DISPATCH BOX 1
MICHAEL   What a relief!

DISPATCH BOX 2
GABRIEL   He's got pancreatic cancer.

ALTAR
MAYA   Order! How long has the Prime Minister
               Angel Michael left to live.

CHANCEL
MARY   He looks terminal to me! Even the church
               today hasn't got it right. They preach con-
               fusion that the past has created.

EVE   Funerals these days are so expensive. Has
                he got an over fifty plan?

DISPATCH BOX 1
MICHAEL   Madam Deputy Speaker! They're going to
                give me three injections. I'll end up with a
                sore bum, and all my hair will fall out.

MAYA moves to the CHANCEL and joins ADAM, EVE
and MARY.

CHANCEL
MARY   Is there such a thing as being a good sin-
                ner? Sex outside of marriage is a sin. I am a
                virgin! No male beast has pushed his body
                inside mine.
ADAM   Yes, but Joseph and Mary were not mar-
                ried when she gave birth in a stable. If she
                had she wouldn't have been a virgin. It is
                us who are sinners together! Why not use
                that sin in ourselves to help mankind?
MAYA   I want Eve and Mary to think of the things
                they did together to overcome and recover
                from their drug addiction.

EVE and MARY face each other HOLDING HANDS.

EVE   Everybody hosts a secret! Search for the se-
                cret inside yourself.

*** MUSIC – APPENDIX 4

LED SCREEN

MARY	EVE
Love is there everywhere	It is true all for you
Love is there everywhere	Seek a grace, track, and trace
Be a star all in all	Love yourself make that call
You will find you're not blind	Love is everywhere

(MARY AND EVE SING)

MARY   I need Madam Deputy Speaker to give me her code of perfection to do something miraculous for this world.

EVE   I'm one of the five thousand who didn't understand.

ADAM   Then let's go back to the bakery.

MAYA   Order! My world of priorities is that we educate the minds of young teenagers. They must all learn to use the paradox of this adventure.

MARY   How do you mean second time?

MAYA   In the beginning it was Adam and Eve that went first and then the Virgin Mary years later. This time you Mary shall go first and establish the Maya Accord with all teenagers on earth. Adam and Eve – you will follow by example with the coming of truth and righteousness as a buzz in the air.

MARY takes hold of MAYA's HAND. ADAM takes hold of EVE's HAND.

ADAM	We are all going to die, but we don't know when.
MAYA	We all have a purpose, but it's knowing what that purpose is. Let the truth be known! As the Virgin Mary I shall lead the way. The coming of the Lord for the second time is nigh.
MARY	Madam Deputy Speaker is real! She can make me buzz anytime.

MAYA and MARY move to the ALTAR TOGETHER. ADAM and EVE move BEFORE the CHANCEL.

ALTAR

MAYA	Order! What is it that helps drug addicts the most when they've had enough, and they want to come back down to earth?
MARY	Madam Deputy Speaker! Computers and iPhones today are a teenager's existence.

DISPATCH BOW 1

MICHAEL	I've just received a text from the hospital. Angel Gabriel is pregnant. His baby like the Goddess of Recovery will not be born of blood or the will of the flesh.

ALTAR

MARY	Order! I would like Madam Deputy Speaker Maya to infuse me with a million megabytes.

DISPATCH BOX 2

GABRIEL	Are we risk takers Madam Deputy Speaker? A baby boy is all we need. A baby girl is very expensive.

ALTAR
MAYA   It's hard for some mothers to understand, but
            when life gets expensive it's because you're
            making the wrong choices.

BEFORE THE CHANCEL
ADAM   We must decide, what are our choices?
EVE   Make a bet with a stranger. Gamble your
            life away.
ADAM   But we're not strangers.

DISPATCH BOX 2
GABRIEL   Madam Deputy Speaker! I just received a
            text from the hospital. Starting tomorrow,
            Angel Michael will undergo his course of
            injections.

DISPATCH BOX 1
MICHAEL   I wonder what colour your baby will be.
            Giving birth is so painful.
ALTAR
MAYA   Order!

BEFORE THE CHANCEL
ADAM   Eve, can you remember months ago – didn't
            we meet at your birthday party?
EVE   I don't think so! Unless! Were you the one
            pretending to be a wolf?
ADAM   Yes! you were pretending to be Snow White
            and you were looking for a man with the
            biggest wallet.
EVE   It was raining!
ADAM   And we ended up in that hotel bar together.

EVE   I'm sober now! It was you! You're the reason I'm now a lesbian and off cocaine.

ALTAR
MARY   Gideon New Testament page 1105.
MAYA   Psalm 31 argues, 'You turned my wailing into dancing, you removed my sackcloth and clothed me in joy.'

*** MUSIC – APPENDIX 3

LED SCREEN

Sickness or in health
In our want and wealth
Seek the truth in prayer
Truth is present everywhere.

TEENAGER CHOIR SINGS with GABRIEL CONDUCTING.

DISPATCH BOX 1
MICHAEL Madam Deputy Speaker! It's terminal! The rugby ball in my belly is getting bigger. Tomorrow I start with the first of three jabs. Will the Leader of the Opposition Angel Gabriel please know I'm not thinking of him either.

ALTAR
MARY   It's too early Maya to start drinking. What say you?

| MAYA | Mary and I are celebrating! She has agreed to be my cherry on a stick! I'll have a spiced rum and coke with a cube of ice. Order! House is suspended for three minutes. |

ANGELS MICHAEL and GABRIEL move to the FRONT of the CHANCEL.

MICHAEL	My head is spinning in the wrong direction. All I can see are babies dancing in the sky!
GABRIEL	We must start believing in the Maya Accord!
MICHAEL	What's the Maya Accord?
GABRIEL	We don't know. It just came about. (puts a hand on his hip)
MICHAEL	With pancreatic cancer I've ended up as a social misfit.
GABRIEL	Most of our YMCA choir spend their spare time in amusement arcades at the bottom of the sea.

BEFORE THE CHANCEL

ADAM	Pancreatic cancer has a cure! All we must do is close our eyes think of Maya and Michael will no longer exist.
EVE	Wow! If that were true what a difference a day makes.
ADAM	There is no stereotyped way of us believing in ourselves.
EVE	I disagree! Mary and I believe!
ADAM	It must be like having a baby! After nine months most young mothers end up with post-natal blues.
EVE	Hell no! Mary is a virgin! The last thing I want is for a man to love me and make me pregnant.

ADAM   Everyone on this Ark has different values
                and speaks different languages. I believe that
                we can all just be good and enjoy each oth-
                er's company.
EVE   I like you, Adam.

ANGELS MICHAEL and GABRIEL go back to their respective DISPATCH BOX.

ALTAR
MARY   But Maya are you saying that mistakes in
                the past don't matter.
MAYA   Order! Is it not true that we learn from mis-
                takes in our past? Mary, for years you have
                simply been off beat, but now you're hit-
                ting the rhythm.
MARY   Being off beat means only seeing things that
                are physically possible. You have opened
                my eyes Maya. I am to live the impossible
                dream.
MAYA   Prime Minister!

DISPATCH BOX 1
MICHAEL   All of you who cannot believe in the im-
                possible have a hardening of their hearts.
                Madam Deputy Speaker! We must all be-
                lieve in the Maya Accord.

DISPATCH BOX 2
GABRIEL   The Maya Accord is set to help us reduce
                the number of drug related deaths through-
                out the world.

DISPATCH BOX 1
MICHAEL   The Maya Accord will reduce unwanted
                 pregnancies and teenager exploitation by
                 drug cartels and abuse.

DISPATCH BOX 2
GABRIEL   The Maya Accord will allow teenagers to
                 make their own personal unimpeded dis-
                 cussions about their own future, based on
                 their own choices.

DISPATCH BOX 1
MICHAEL   In fact the Maya Accord has a myriad of ben-
                 efits for the youngsters of today that will for-
                 ever influence their future accomplishments.

ALTA
MAYA   Order! Will somebody please make me aware
                 of the Maya Accord minutes.

BEFORE THE CHANCEL
ADAM   We must believe in the power of the Maya
                 Accord and teach it to the world.
EVE   The Maya Accord is like a musical tune
                 you can dance to. Love only creates a baby,
                 but the Maya Accord turns that baby into a
                 healthy 'let's do it again' scenario.

ALTAR
MAYA   Prime Minister!

DISPATCH BOX 1
MICHAEL   The Maya Accord is a buzz that a couple can
                 experience, a buzz that rocks the Ark Baby!

GABRIEL   It's a buzz that beats all the other kicks and
               buzzes a teenager can get in this life.

ALTAR
MAYA   Order! Am I missing something? I can't see
               the wood for the trees!
MARY   Here are the minutes. Maya – have a read!
               (gives MAYA several books). We can practise
               it together during the interval. I shall reveal
               everything, and Madam Deputy Speaker
               will commend the Virgin Mary at work to
               the house.
MAYA   Is it akin to love?
MARY   No love is the opposite! Love makes babies!

BEFORE THE CHANCEL
EVE   It's not what a pillow gives but rather what
               it takes. Away.
ADAM   Are we not supposed to love each other?
               like the love thy neighbour bit!
EVE   That's love from yesterday! Love today is
               making babies.

*** MUSIC – APPENDIX 10

LED SCREEN
EVE   ADAM
Sing a song   Eternal paradise
All day long   Heavenly word
Like the moon   Eternal Paradise
Sing in tune   Heavenly joy

Make your bet	Creations unending call
Race with sin	
Close your eyes	Glorious seed
Dreams will win	Does grow

EVE   Yes! Today a boy meets a girl, their infatuation is not love, their bodies take over their minds. They lose control and suffer the consequences.

ADAM So their love for each other is just sex.

EVE   No! Sex is something completely different. It is the false love of today that causes many pregnancies to end up in abortions, abuse, and social illness.

ADAM Such love today causes wars, murders, and untold grief.

EVE   The worst thing is that young people turn to drugs as a way out.

ALTAR

MARY So teenagers who have not yet gained their feet must avoid love at all costs.

MAYA I couldn't have put it better myself. Order! There are some things in life that all men enjoy. Prime Minister!

DISPATCH BOX 1

MICHAEL I fail to see how the Angel Gabriel and I can improve on what I enjoy the most.

DISPATCH BOX 2

GABRIEL Madam Deputy Speaker! We both enjoy your righteousness and the truth according to your word. Please confirm in our minds your understanding of the situation.

DISPATCH BOX 1

MICHAEL   Madam Deputy Speaker! Isn't it amazing!
                 When does Angel Gabriel's pillow become
                 a real baby?

ALTAR

MARY   Your infatuation for each other is part of
                 the Maya Accord.

MAYA   Does it take three to tango! Order!

BEFORE THE CHANCEL

ADAM   Who was drunk and woke up in the wrong
                 bed?

EVE   Last time the Virgin Mary gave birth was in
                 a manger, but this time it's going to be on a
                 city highway in the back of a car.

ADAM   That's the norm these days for many mothers.
                 (looks at EVE's body).

EVE   I put forward the idea that if your eyes cause
                 you to sin then close them.

ALTAR

MAYA   Order! Gideon New Testament 2009 page
                 240. Mark argues 'If your eye causes you to
                 sin, pluck it out. It is better for you to enter
                 the kingdom of God with one eye than to
                 have two eyes and be thrown into hell.'

MARY   But it's understanding what it means Maya
                 that is more important.

MAYA	MARY
Lucifer my brother is the father of sin.	So what does that mean?

| MARY | It means you must learn to live with sin by turning it into something useful. |
| MAYA | I shall create from sin an action plan to clean up this sordid world. |

DISPATCH BOX 2
| GABRIEL | Madam Deputy Speaker! Will my baby have horns, pointed ears, a dagger like tail and razor- sharp teeth? |

DISPATCH BOX 1
| MICHAEL | Only if it's a baby girl! She'll grow up spitting fire and tempting boys in the long grass. |

ALTAR
| MAYA | Order! |

DISPATCH BOX 2
| GABRIEL | Madam Deputy Speaker! She'll wrap all men around her little finger. |

DISPATCH BOX 1
| MICHAEL | That's a good idea! |

MAYA move to the NAVE
MARY moves to the CHANCEL
ANGELS MICHAEL and GABRIEL move to the CONGREGATION

NAVE
| MAYA | There are five pieces in my jigsaw that you must find and put together. |

CONGREGATION
MICHAEL   What's your jigsaw about? Is it physical or
             is it spiritual?

NAVE
MAYA   Both! Five ways of life depict mankind's
             destiny. Guess what that destiny is?

ADAM and EVE, HOLDING HANDS, move to the
CHANCEL and join MARY
ANGELS MICHAEL and GABRIEL move BEFORE the
CHANCEL.

CHANCEL
MARY   Does it have anything to do with the mean-
             ing of love?

NAVE
MAYA   Yes! No more clues!

BEFORE THE CHANCEL
MICHAEL   Are we talking about givers or takers?
GABRIEL   Are we talking about deceivers or receivers?

CHANCEL
ADAM   But we're not deceivers!
EVE   Do the pieces of your jigsaw turn into a
             graveyard?
ADAM   With a tomb of doom for drug addicts.
MARY   What is the meaning of those pieces?

BEFORE THE CHANCEL
MICHAEL   Is the first piece a devil reaper swinging a
             scythe and cutting into piles of dead bodies.

GABRIEL	Is the second piece, a stiff body protruding from a coffin?

CHANCEL

EVE	Is the third piece a hangman's noose swinging in the wind?
ADAM	A chopping block surrounded by buckets of mutilated bodies and heads.
MARY	But what is the fifth? Could it be a bowl of salt, a loaf of bread or a wooden cross?

NAVE

MAYA	No! You're all wrong! It is you who are the pieces. You are all just one colour, but when I put you together you form a rainbow. This is the end of your rainbow, and all teenagers will find the Maya Accord treasure.

*** MUSIC — APPENDIX 5

MAYA PLAYS a TROBONE SOLO

MARY moves to the NAVE and joins MAYA

MARY	A fountain of light has come about. Angel Michael's pancreatic cancer doesn't stand a chance.

CHANCEL

EVE	I'm wind surfing through the seas of outer space. I'd much rather have sex with a man.

ADAM   We shall surf forever through time together.

EVE   Never say die! Everything is within our
                heads. Find and experience the Maya Accord
                and you'll never steer out of control.

ADAM   Find yourself spinning into a glorious future.

NAVE

MAYA   If it works, we have the ammunition to start
                again.

MARY   I'm going to show you a narrow gate that
                becomes a highway to heaven.

MAYA   Order! Order! Will the Prime Minister make
                a statement to the house?

BEFORE THE CHANCEL

MICHAEL   Madam Deputy Speaker! Everybody has a
                terminal illness. They call it old age.

GABRIEL   So let's us enjoy life while we're young! Eve
                will be the people's princess.

CHANCEL

ADAM   We're not dead yet. We mustn't die and be
                just a bad smell.

NAVE

MAYA   Order! Leader of the Opposition!

BEFORE THE CHANCEL

GABRIEL   Madam Deputy Speaker! Angel Michael
                has pancreatic cancer, must we believe in
                the truth?

MICHAEL   Madam Deputy Speaker! Is there a cure?
                Can my body overcome a pancreatic death
                sentence?

GABRIEL	No! You can't give me what I need any more.

NAVE

MAYA	Order!
MARY	It's no longer about what happens now, but rather what doesn't happen in the future.

CHANCEL

ADAM	Our Maya Accord will take away all our doubts.
EVE	I have no doubts.
ADAM	A veil has been torn in two!
EVE	Gideon New Testament 2009 page 889.
ADAM	Hebrews 2 argues 'I shall declare your name to my brothers; in the presence of the congregation, I shall sing your praise.'

*** MUSIC — APPENDIX 7

LED SCREEN

Oh, praise our Lord on high!
Our love has reached the sky!
With everlasting grace
We sing like stars in space
TEENAGE CHOIR SINGS

BEFORE THE CHANCEL

MICHAEL	I can feel my rugby ball moving within me. It keeps getting bigger and bigger.

NAVE

MARY	Something unbelievable is happening inside everyone. Laws of the past and social taboos I shall fling out the window.
MAYA	Shall I kick Angel Michael's rugby ball into touch?
MARY	Perhaps it never existed.

CHANCEL

ADAM	Why do women always look at their man as if he's done something wrong?
EVE	I forgive you.
ADAM	Who are you kidding! We still don't really know each other.
EVE	Don't rush me! I want to get things right this time.

ANGELS MICHAEL and GABRIEL move to their respective DISPATCH BOXES.
ADAM and EVE move BEFORE the CHANCEL.

DISPATCH BOX 1

MICHAEL	Madam Deputy Speaker! I'm looking for a planet of wealth and good fortune.

DISPATCH BOX 2

GABRIEL	We're both lost sheep in an intangible dimension.

DISPATCH BOX 1

MICHAEL	When's the next train?

DISPATCH BOX 2
GABRIEL   First stop! Shall we introduce our teenager
               choir to debauchery and suffering, or not?

DISPATCH BOX 1
MICHAEL   No! tomorrow I shall be in hospital.

BEFORE THE CHANCEL
EVE   You're my best friend. I feel like I've known
               you for ages.
ADAM   Let's add a square to a square and make a
               rectangle.
EVE   Correct! But if I add my thoughts as a cir-
               cle, to your rectangle, it becomes a lock.
ADAM   Our Maya Accord is the key to our lock.
EVE   There will be only one key for my lock and
               that is you.

NAVE
MAYA   I have had a dream! I had a gold head, sil-
               ver shoulders, brass body, copper legs and
               clay feet. Can you interpret this dream for
               me Mary?
MARY   Yes! Angel Gabriel is to go for a check-up
               at the hospital. He starts as gold; when he
               gets to the hospital, he'll be silver; while
               he's waiting for his check-up, he'll be brass;
               when he goes in for his check-up, he'll be
               copper; when he comes out he will be clay.

EXIT MAYA HOLDING HANDS with MARY.

*** MUSIC – APPENDIX 6

LED SCREEN
I feel so bad, be a good sinner
Give us your story, your race you will win
Saved by his bell, mighty ringer
Sounding together with fury akin.
Know the truth! Know the truth!
Know the truth! Make your life work.
Know the truth! Know the truth!
Know the truth do!
I feel so bad, be a good sinner
Give us your story, your race you will win
Love is forever! Love is forever! Love is forever! True!
(TEENAGE CHOIR SINGS)

ANGELS MICHAEL, GABRIEL and the TEENAGE CHOIR move BEFORE the CHANCEL and join ADAM and EVE.

ACT TWO

SET – ARK
CHANCEL
ENTER MARY with a TRUMPET and MAYA with a
TROMBONE and with their BACKS TO EACH OTHER,
PLAY a DUET

*** MUSIC – APPENDIX 1

MAYA and MARY move to the ALTAR.

*** MUSIC – APPENDIX 2

LED SCREEN

City of hope hear our plea	Come gracious Lord
Give us your word	Sing heavenly King
Help us see	Light and Love
Teach us true we are so blue	O set us free
Give us your grace in this place	With a true love be

ENTER PROCESSION SINGING – TEENAGE CHOIR
waving BANNERS and FLAGS; EVE as a graduates wearing CAP and GOWN with ADAM as CHOIR MASTER,
and ANGEL MICHAEL and GABRIEL as NUNS wearing HABITS following behind.

TEENAGE CHOIR splits into two and they go either side
of ADAM and MAYA on the CHANCEL, to their respec-
tive CHOIR PEWS.
ANGEL MICHAEL and GABRIEL go to their respective
DISPATCH BOX
ADAM and EVE stand BEFORE THE CHANCEL

ALTAR

MARY	It will help put an end to teenage aggression.
MAYA	How do you mean?
MARY	Young men all have a possessive aggression for things they own and value; for things they think they own and for things they have the potential of owning. Violence is part of their human nature. Knife crime and drugs, with teenagers dismembering and cutting each other up, is a pointless part of community life. These days, death is commonplace on the streets.
MAYA	Possessive territorial aggression!
MARY	In other words, they don't get a buzz out of life, they fall victim to violent drug dealers and crime.
MAYA	This is heavy stuff!
MARY	Then we must reduce the impact it is having on society and community life, by teaching the Maya Accord to kids in schools.
MAYA	You have a valid point!
MARY	Did you not enjoy the Maya Accord?
MAYA	You only gave me parts one and two, and I was drifting into another dimension.

DISPATCH BOX 2
GABRIEL   Madam Deputy Speaker! Which one of your
                 worlds are we living in?

DISPATCH BOX 1
MICHAEL   What's it like in hell?

DISPATCH BOX 2
GABRIEL   Madam Deputy Speaker! Why did you make
                 Angel Michael look pregnant when he's not?

ALTAR
MAYA   Think! Which is the richest world in the
                 kingdom of heaven?
MARY   It will be the one where the Maya Accord
                 is a part of life.
MAYA   You must all catch a train and get off when
                 you hear bells ringing. I'll be the train driver!

BEFORE THE CHANCEL
ADAM   Let's give it a go Eve! Mary can get into the
                 first carriage with Angels Michael and Gabriel
                 and we'll get into the second carriage.

MARY, MICHAEL, and GABRIEL move to the
CHANCEL/FIRST CARRIAGE

FIRST CARRIAGE
MARY   This first carriage is approaching a planet
                 of persecution.
MICHAEL   Keep going!
GABRIEL   Oh no! The worst has happened! There
                 was a big mix up with our paperwork at the
                 hospital. Our medical notes got mixed up

	and put on the wrong clip board. It's Angel Michael who's pregnant!

and put on the wrong clip board. It's Angel
Michael who's pregnant!

Michael's pancreatic cancer papers are mine.
One of your world's mistakes! – Madam
Deputy Speaker; it must be a betrayal.

MICHAEL   Everyone makes mistakes! Angel Gabriel
will die sooner than most.

ALTAR

MAYA   Can we sing?

MARY   I am going on a train first class to the gar-
den of Eden. I shall marry Joseph just before I go into labour. As a married virgin I
shall give birth to a son.

MAYA   Your train is due to arrive before the chancel.
Your first-class carriage as the Old Testament
is followed by a second-class carriage or New
Testament for Adam and Eve.

BEFORE CHANCEL

EVE   Gideon New Testament 2009 page 344.

ADAM   Luke 11 argues 'Blessed is the mother who
gave you birth and nursed you.'

*** MUSIC – APPENDIX 7

LED SCREEN
My Holy Spirit be
A gracious olive tree
Your words that help and heal.
Oh teach Thy Grace to me
TEENAGE CHOIR SINGS

MAYA and MARY moves BEFORE THE CHANCEL/
MARKED TRAIN ENGINE – FIRST CLASS – SECOND
CLASS

FIRST CLASS
MARY   They call this train the beginning and the
            end! Don't you see like Maya that the be-
            ginning is the end, and the end is the be-
            ginning. I am now in the first carriage in-
            stead of the second.

DISPATCH BOX 1
MICHAEL   Division! Your planet Gabriel is the planet
            of pestilence. This journey is going to be
            fun. I need to put my feet up. I'm pregnant.

DISPATCH BOX 2
GABRIEL   We need to sit with the congregation.

ANGELS MICHAEL and GABRIEL move and SIT WITH
the CONGREGATION

SECOND CLASS
EVE   Mary doesn't turn me on anymore. I'd much
            rather you and me get to know each other
            in this second carriage.

CONGREGATION
GABRIEL   The surgeons are going to operate! I'm too
            far gone for injections.
MICHAEL   I've ordered flowers for your funeral and
            got a discount.

FIRST CARRIAGE
MARY   The congregation must get off the train at
               the planet of forgiveness.

TRAIN ENGINE
MAYA   What shall I do? Mary is sure to need both
               Angels Michael and Gabriel when she reach-
               es Bethlehem. Angel Gabriel is going to be
               derailed at the breakers yard.

CONGREGATION
MICHAEL   Madam Deputy Speaker! You must rocket
               Angel Gabriel to a planet of famine; a tac-
               tic of delay to slow down the growth of his
               pancreatic fate.

SECOND CLASS
EVE   That will only prolong the pain.

CONGREGATION
MICHAEL   Angel Gabriel has a dying wish before he
               stops breathing.
GABRIEL   Surgeons are going to slice me in two and
               rip my belly out and if there are any grisly
               bits they'll use a chain saw. But not to wor-
               ry they said they'd staple me back together.

SECOND CLASS
ADAM   Angel Michael could be a fortune teller.

FIRST CLASS
MARY   Let the world sing for the Angel Gabriel.

SECOND CARRIAGE

EVE   Gideon New Testament 2009 page 1003.

ADAM   Revelation 7 argues 'Salvation belongs to our engine driver, that sits on the throne.' (points at Maya)

*** MUSIC – APPENDIX 8

LED SCREEN

Take my bone and let them be
Swift or peaceful just for thee.
Take my voice and let me sing
Only for my King
(MICHAEL SINGS)

We send a message with a kiss
From our lips your words we wish
Take our voice and let us sing
Only for our King
(GABRIEL SINGS)

CONGREGATION

GABRIEL   Don't listen to Angel Michael! We're all bangers waiting to go bang! One day soon we shall all believe in ourselves.

SECOND CLASS

EVE   Just think! The first time this happened Mary had her baby in a stable, then she got married in Egypt.

FIRST CLASS
MARY   But not this time! I shall marry Joe in the
              first two minutes before I have my baby, as
              a virgin. It won't be a mysterious revelation
              anymore.

SECOND CLASS
ADAM   Eve, you represent the truth. We could get
              married first before you bite into the apple.
EVE   The word common law has many meanings.
              For many today, wedlock is just a piece of
              paper so migrants can stay in this country.
              All I need is your undying respect.
ADAM   We are teenagers of today who just need to
              be shown physical eutopia.

CONGREGATION
GABRIEL   Mary, did you not kiss your train driver
              Maya on her lips?

FIRST CARRIAGE
MARY   Yes! I kissed her cheek first!

SECOND CLASS
EVE   Was it just a friendship kiss?

FIRST CLASS
MARY   Believing in the truth is a bit like post-natal-
              depression. It's something you can't change.

CONGREGATION
GABRIEL   Who believes that kissing the train drive on
              the cheek has made Mary pregnant?

MICHAEL   I believe it was the train driver that kissed
               Mary first.

FIRST CLASS
MAYA   Was it me that said a kiss is but a kiss? A
               smile is but a smile!

SECOND CARRIAGE
EVE   Maya as Goddess of Recovery is to be sus-
               pended with immediate effect. She is obvi-
               ously responsible for making Mary pregnant.

FIRST CLASS
MAYA   Next stop is planet Earth. Fasten your seat
               belts. It is sure to be a rough landing.

MAYA, MARY, ADAM and EVE move to the CHANCEL

CHANCEL
MARY   Everyone is to be young at heart. If you
               want to believe in something holy, it's your
               choice. You will still feel the pains of every-
               day life, but the Maya Accord will be your
               foundation and you'll someday be a born-
               again Christian.
MAYA,   You have work to do Mary. I'll be a shep-
               herd and find you a manger. Adam and Eve
               have got to find their fountain in an orchard.
               Angels Michael and Gabriel have just got to
               look good!
MARY   This time when I get to planet Earth I shall
               make way for Adam and Eve. This time the
               Maya Accord is going to make life incred-
               ibly enjoyable.

CONGREGATION

MICHAEL   There is a world of youth in the congrega-
           tions who want to see the Maya Accord in
           action.

GABRIEL   We must remove the pestilence of mankind
           that is mingled with scripture.

MICHAEL   Crime in this life is like pouring petrol onto
           an open fire.

GABRIEL   It will be wonderful when the Maya Accord
           runs hand in hand with our righteousness.

MICHAEL   What would you say if I said it will save so-
           ciety billions of pounds?

GABRIEL   Many social workers won't have to work so
           hard.

CHANCEL

EVE   What would you say if I said I once lived
           with a ferry captain?

ADAM   Don't say that. People will think you're shop-
           soiled. Our new Maya Accord is a healthy
           way for teenagers and community devel-
           opment. We ourselves are the result of our
           mother and father loving each other.

EVE   All men are ugly creatures. A lot forget to
           wash under their arm pits. I hope you keep
           your body clean.

ADAM   This world is like being on probation. Above
           is heaven and below is hell. It's a continu-
           um that helps us learn from our mistakes.

*** MUSIC — APPENDIX 7

LED SCREEN

My holy Spirit be
A light that shines on me
And with thy wisdom true
I spend my life with you.
(TEENAGE CHOIR SINGS)

MAYA	Everyone here will feel themselves shaking hands with my diadem of grace.
MARY	So that's how you made me pregnant!

CONGREGATION

MICHAEL	Today love is thought of as a three-letter word.
GABRIEL	We're all waiting for you to go into labour.
MICHEAL	Would you like to hear its heartbeat? (points at his pillow).

CHANCEL

EVE	All girls ought to be virgins up until they want to have a baby.
ADAM	But we know that most young girls want to find out who they are before that!
EVE	They must all be taught to copy the Virgin Mary.
ADAN	But no boy when young likes being told what to do.
EVE	I say give them the choice. Put this Maya Accord on the table, let them decide.

ADAM	All institutional establishments of today consider love outside of marriage to be a sin.
EVE	All young girls consider love to mean making babies.
ADAM	It does, they are right! Why do religious establishments encourage young teenagers to love each other?
EVE	As soon as I found my buzz in life there was no stopping me. I ended up having a miscarriage because I didn't then understand how my body worked; I ended up on drugs.
ADAM	Young teenagers need to be taught the explicit truth. We must all learn to enjoy our bodies but in a safe way.
EVE	Then I met the Virgin Mary and here I am.
ADAM	We shall decide! All teenagers like us from now on are to experience the Maya Accord and be left to choose for themselves.

ANGEL MICHAEL and GABRIEL move BEFORE THE CHANCEL

BEFORE THE CHANCEL

| GABRIEL | We all must make the right choice. Do we want to live a life or die a death? |
| Michael | Some may choose to remain sinless and lie on a bed of nails. |

ANGELS MICHAEL and GABRIEL move to their respective DISPATCH BOX.

CHANCEL

| ADAM | According to some scriptures, our life is written before we are born. |

*** MUSIC – APPENDIX 9

LED SCREEN

ADAM	EVE
I do no wrong	Pretence! Pretence! Pretence!
I sing this song	Pretence!
I serve my country	Sin is for sinners
all day long	who live a lie
Truth is for winners	We make mistakes
who do not die	we choose our fate.
Love is divine	Give your time

DISPATCH BOX 1

MICHAEL   My own scripture is one big spelling mistake.

DISPATCH BOX 2

GABRIEL   Will the Angel Michael admit to this house that the Maya Accord originated from the elongated heads of Egyptian Pharaohs.

DISPATCH BOX 1

MICHAEL   Will the Angel Gabriel admit that my elongation is bigger than his.

DISPATCH BOX 2

GABRIEL   Will the Angel Michael let us know why he made the wrong choice.

DISPATCH BOX 1

MICHAEL   Could it be that the Angel Gabriel made the Virgin Mary pregnant with the intention of finding Joseph to cover the cost.

MAYA and MARY move to NAVE

NAVE

MAYA   It is undoubtedly clear that social dishonesty
              in this world influences even Angels from
              above.

MARY   Forget the poor! Religion makes more mon-
              ey out of the rich aristocracy.

ADAM moves to a PULPIT on one side of the CHANCEL
and EVE moves to a PULPIT on the other side

PULPIT 1

ADAM   We as teenagers all need a penicillin jab with
              a yearly booster.

PULPIT 2

EVE   Disease in general would be halved overnight.

PULPIT 1

ADAM   Just think of the money we could redirect
              on education.

PULPIT 2

EVE   The benefits of the Maya Accord are immense.

DISPATCH BOX 2

GABRIEL   Our lives have become bipolar!

DISPATCH BOX 1

MICHAEL   The values teenagers have been taught in
              the past are old fashioned. Past ideas need
              to go up a gear to keep up with the times.

DISPATCH BOX 2
GABRIEL   It's too late for Adam! Accusations have been
             made and his feathers are tarnished.
MICHAEL   Society in general believes in social justice.
             You can do what you want in this world,
             but if you tell anyone or drop your guard,
             it becomes a crime.

ADAM and EVE; ANGELS MICHAEL and GABRIEL
all move to the CHANCEL

CHANCEL
ADAM   We shall all now live again.
EVE   Gideon New Testament 2009 page 807.
MICHAEL   Ephesians 9 argues, 'Wake up, O sleeper,
             rise from the dead, and salvation will shine
             on you.'

*** MUSIC – APPENDIX 7

LED SCREEN

Oh, mighty Spirit be
A mighty force in me
To win my steeple chase
Oh, bless me with Thy Grace
TEENAGE CHOIR SINGS

NAVE
MAYA   I'm not sure what it is but I'm going to open
             a large bottle of champagne.

CHANCEL

EVE   Charity at its best is when a woman gives
             her love to a man.
GABRIEL   Does Eve love Adam? Is she not looking for
             a man who's got a job, a house, a yacht, a
             fast car, and plenty of money?
EVE   That's not true!
ADAM   If a man and woman don't love each other,
             they shouldn't have children and get married.
MICHAEL   But then the Maya Accord is at its best.
ADAM   It's all in the mind.
EVE   Lust is one of the deadly sins.

NAVE

MARY   Sapphires come in a range of colours.
MAYA   Will the congregation point us in the right
             direction.

CHANCEL

EVE   So do dead bodies.

NAVE

MARY   When your circulation stops you will become
             one of those cool holy ghosts. The colour of
             your sapphire is the colour of your stockings.
MAYA   You're all standing on the wing of an airplane
             flying high in the sky. Nobody is wearing
             a parachute.

CHANCEL

EVE   How come Satan has ten heads and they're
             all different colours.
MICHAEL   The colour of our skin makes us physically
             perfect.

EVE   No man is physically perfect.

NAVE
MARY   You should know!
MAYA   As the level of faith in who you are goes up,
               so does the colour of your stockings.
MARY   Your aeroplane has turned upside down and
               everyone here is in freefall.
MAYA   Let the fun begin!

CHANCEL
MICHAEL   But I don't wear stockings!
GABRIEL   Less to take off when we go to bed.

NAVE
MARY   What colour are my stockings? (undresses
               to reveal green stockings)
MAYA   That colour green means you're all systems
               go.

CHANCEL
GABRIEL   Eve's stockings are sure to be overflowing
               with sinful thoughts.
MICHAEL   Her secrets of the past.
EVE   You can show me yours if you want, but
               I'm going to take mine off.

ADAM and EVE, HOLDING HANDS, disappear behind
a CHURCH PEW

MICHAEL   What's the colour of your stockings?
GABRIEL   Who am I? (undresses to reveal pink stock-
               ings with blue spots)
MICHAEL   Pink stockings with blue spots!

GABRIEL	Blue spots can't be mine. They belong to you!
MICHAEL	I'll soon find out! (undresses to reveal yellow stockings with question marks).

NAVE
| MARY | Yellow stockings with question marks! |

FEMALE SCREAM from behind CHURCH PEW

ADAM and EVE undressed; move on to the CHANCEL, both holding up a pair of RED STOCKINGS.

CHANCEL
| EVE | I'm not wearing them! |
| ADAM | We're definitely not red! |

NAVE
| MAYA | Have you got a contingency plan? |
| MARY | Leave it to me! |

MARY runs BEFORE the CHANCEL and passes both ADAM and EVE a pair of WHITE STOCKINGS; ADAM and EVE FOR ALL TO SEE put their WHITE STOCKINGS ON.

CHANCEL
| GABRIEL | Now we know who we are, we can all touch elbows. |

NAVE
| MAYA | You are all going to hit a trampoline, so keep your legs together. You will all bounce to where you're supposed to be. |

ANGELS MICHAEL and GABRIEL move to the FRONT
of the CHANCEL.

CHANCEL
GABRIEL   Perhaps Adam and Eve can give us more
               insight into the Maya Accord?

ADAM and EVE in their WHITE STOCKINGS move
BEFORE THE CHANCEL

BEFORE THE CHANCEL
EVE   If I tell you Adam will you promise not to
               hate me?
ADAM   Is it that serious?
EVE   Yes! Mary and I were Lesbians for a rea-
               son. Had I known about the Maya Accord
               before taking drugs I wouldn't have taken
               drugs in the first place.

*** MUSIC – APPENDIX 3

LED SCREEN

Heads and heels and toes
A time of love does grow.
With helping hands in prayer
Truth is present everywhere
TEENAGE CHOIR SINGS with GABRIEL CONDUC-
TING

EVE moves to the FRONT of the CHANCEL.

ANGELS MICHAEL and GABRIEL move and Join ADAM
BEFORE THE CHANCEL

BEFORE THE CHANCEL
ADAM   Tell us more!

CHANCEL
EVE   KY is a lubricant that you can buy in all
                chemists. It's not just a lubricant it's germ
                free, removes surface bacteria and comes in
                different flavours.

BEFORE THE CHANCEL
GABRIEL   We like the strawberry flavour.

CHANCEL
EVE   KY is used by mothers when breast feeding
                a baby. She rubs it on her areola and nipples
                profusely.

BEFORE THE CHANCEL
MICHAEL   Profusely!

CHANCEL
EVE   A mother uses KY to clean away surface bac-
                teria and helps to prevent her nipples get-
                ting sore. Her baby with lips on the moth-
                er's nipple tastes the strawberry flavour, licks
                away, and begins to suck.

BEFORE THE CHANCEL
ADAM   A baby tastes the mothers nipple, then for ap-
                proximately five seconds sucks on the areola

around that nipple, causing it to go back and forth in and out of the baby's mouth.

CHANCEL
EVE   Then the baby resting, with its tongue licking the mother's nipple for three seconds, starts all over again. First licking the protruding nipple for three seconds and then sucking on the areola again and again. Don't you see? Forget the milk and replace the baby with a partner. The Maya Accord comes in three parts this is the first.

BEFORE THE CHANCEL
ADAM   Please continue!
MICHAEL   Tell me something I don't know!
GABRIEL   Will you give us a live demonstration?

CHANCEL
EVE   The second part of the Maya Accord is the same procedure again and again except this time it's not a mother's nipple but in the same way, a nipple becomes my clitoris. My mother used to call it my 'tootsie'. The buzz a woman gets is magnified again and again until the buzz is continuous.

NAVE
MAYA   And what is the third part?
MARY   The third part is a woman KY-ing a man standing erect, and that man KY-ing his woman's bum.

BEFORE THE CHANCEL
GABRIEL   Heavens be we've been undone.

ANGELS MICHAEL and GABRIEL look at each other.

MICHAEL   I have to find a woman to try it out.

ADAM moves joining EVE at the FRONT of the CHANCEL

CHANCEL
ADAM   This could be the dawning of a new age!
EVE   Young teenagers are to stop losing and to
               start winning.
ADAM   Young teenagers don't have to worry about
               false babies but should rather just focus on
               growing up.
EVE   Teenagers can control pregnancy, so a preg-
               nancy doesn't control them.

BEFORE THE CHANCEL
MICHAEL   The Goddess of recovery , she's definitely
               got a monstrous 'tootsie'.
GABRIEL   Yes! Let's celebrate who we are. Freedom
               at last!
MICHAEL   Tomorrow it will be his bald man in a boat.
GABRIEL   We have been given a transgender solution.

NAVE
MAYA   There are lots of onlookers in the dark,
               dodging around trying to hide the colour
               of their stockings.

BEFORE THE CHANCEL

MICHAEL   Get real! Sucking a devil's doorbell or sugar plum is to be a new norm.

GABRIEL   Adam's pearl is Eve's sweet spot. Who has a love button ladies. Be your man's hooded lady.

CHANCEL

EVE   If you're wearing transparent stockings it's because you haven't tried about the Maya Accord.

ADAM   We shall share our white stockings with you.

BEFORE THE CHANCEL

GABRIEL   Let us all learn to enjoy our lives.

ADAM and EVE joining MATA and MARY move to the NAVE

NAVE

ADAM   Why should we care about others. As long as we know the Maya Accord's secret, who cares about those who can't see past their noses.

MARY   Joseph, where are you Joseph? I need a man to marry me!

EVE   Adam! Will you be my babe, make me buzz! I'll KY you if you KY me. (puts her finger on ADAMS lips).

MAYA   A dream come true!

LED SCREEN

I feel so bad, be a good sinner
Give us your story, your race you will win
Saved by his bell, mighty ringer
Sounding together with fury akin.
Know the truth! Know the truth! Know the truth!
Make your life work!
Know the truth! Know the truth! Know the truth do!
I feel so bad, be a good sinner
Give us your story, your race you will win.
Love is forever! Love is forever! Love is forever! True!
TEENAGER CHOIR SING as they move to the NAVE

LED SCREEN
THE END

ADAM and EVE, ANGELS MICHAEL and GABRIEL
move to NAVE and join MAYA, MARY and TEENAGE
CHOIR
PROCESSION with BANNERS, FLAGS and CANDLES
FORMS AT NAVE

LED SCREEN

High in the heavens above
Goodness and glory shine
God's love is true, truth does break through
Fountains of grace for you
Sweet breath of heavenly joy
Wisdom and wonders above
God's love to be church sets us free
Maya Accord helps you see

EXIT PROCESSION.

APPENDIX

Appendix 1   Trumpet and Trombone Duet

Appendix 1

Appendix 2

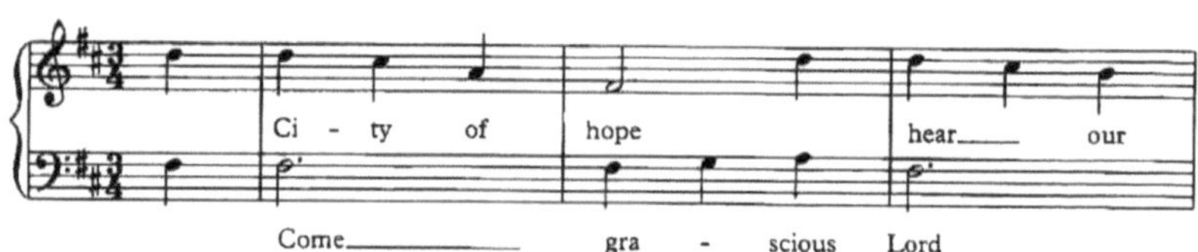

Ci - ty of hope hear our
Come gra - scious Lord

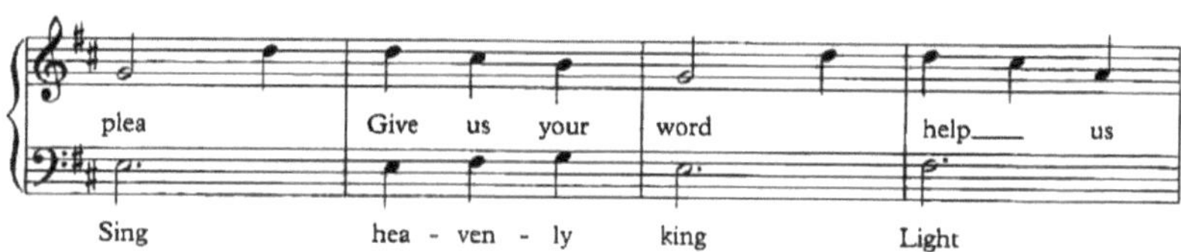

plea Give us your word help us
Sing hea - ven - ly king Light

see Teach us true we are so
and love o set

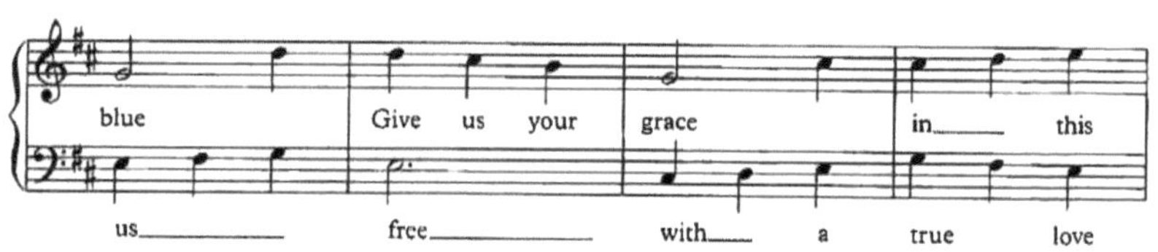

blue Give us your grace in this
us free with a true love

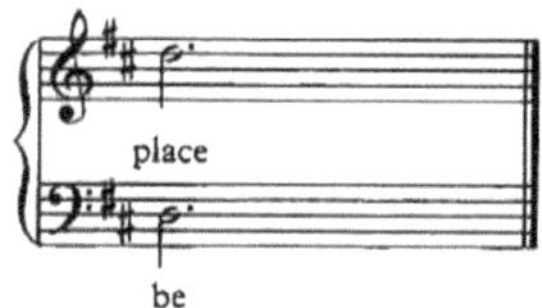

place
be

Appendix 3

1. Seek the throne of grace
2. Sick - ness or in health
3. Heads and hearts and toes
It's in ev - ery place
In our want and wealth
A time of love does grow
When we live in prayer
Seek the truth in prayer
With help - ing hands in prayer
Truth is pre - sent ev - ery - where.
Truth is pre - sent ev - ery - where.
Truth is pre - sent ev - ery - where.

Appendix 4

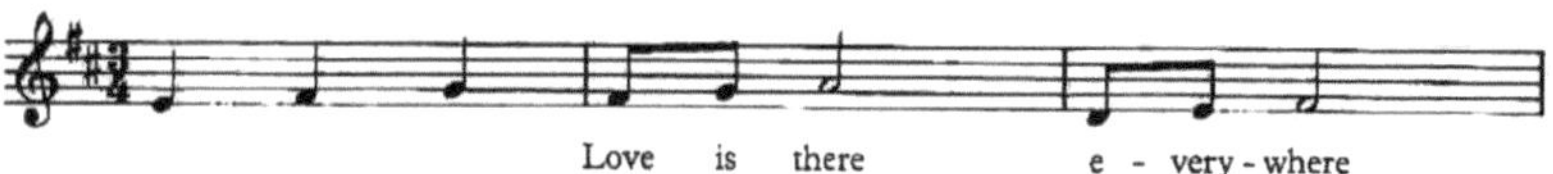

Love   is   there   e - very - where

It   is   true   all   for   you   Love   is   there

e - very - where   seek   a   grace   track   and   trace

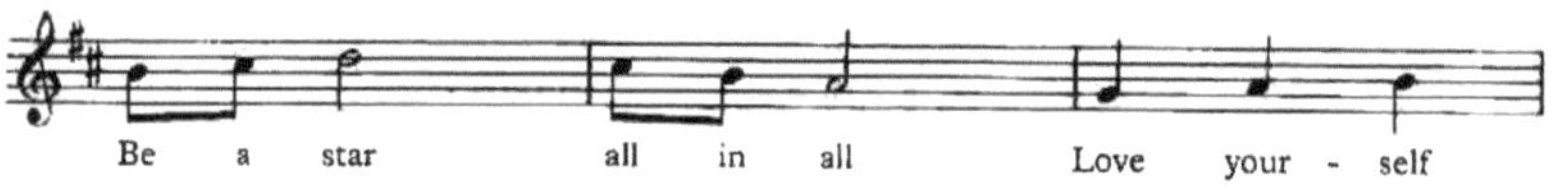

Be   a   star   all   in   all   Love   your - self

make   that   call   You   will   find   you're   not   blind

Love   is   eve - ry - where

Appendix 5
Trombone Solo
71

Appendix 6

I feel so bad, be a good sin - ner Give us your sto - ry, your
race you will win Saved by our bell, migh - ty a ring - er
Sound-ing to - geth - er with fu - ry a - kin Know the truth!
Know the truth! Know the truth! Make your life work!
Know the truth! Know the truth! Know the truth!
Do! I feel so bad, be a good sin - ner
Give us your sto - ry, your race you will win Love is for - ev - er!
Love is for - ev - er! Love is for - ev - er! True!

Appendix 7

1. My
2. My
3. Oh
4. Oh

Ho - ly Spi - rit be   A   gra - cious o - live
Ho - ly Spi - rit be   A   light   that shines   on
migh - ty Spi - rit be   A   migh - ty force   in
praise our Lord on high Our love   has reached the

tree   Your Words that help   and heal   Oh
me   And   with   Thy wis - dom true   I
me   To   win   my stee - ple chase Oh
sky   With ev -   er - last - ing grace We

teach Thy grace to me.
spend my life with you.
bless me with Thy grace.
sing like stars in space.

Appendix 8

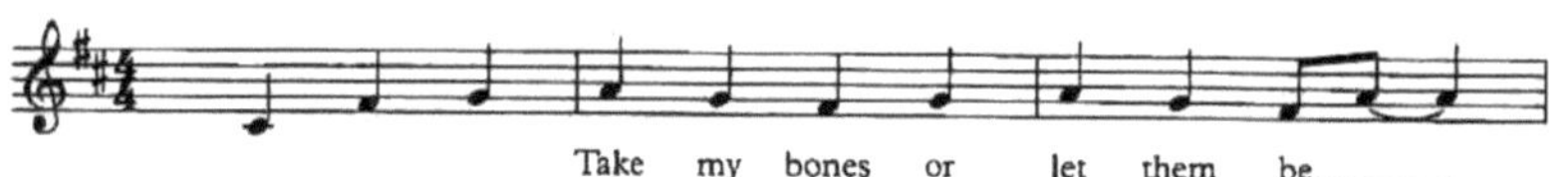
Take my bones or let them be

Swift or peace - ful just for thee Take my voice and

let me sing On - ly for my King We

send a mes - sage with a kiss From our lips your

words we wish Take our voice and let us sing

On - ly for our king

Appendix 9

I do no wrong I sing this song
Pre - tence
Pre - tence
I serve my coun - try all day long
Pre - tence Pre - tence Sin is for sin - ners that
live a lie
Truth is for win - ners who do not die
We
make mis - takes we choose our fate
Love
Give your time
so di -vine

Appendix 10

Sing a song
E - ter - nal pa - ra - dise hea - ven - ly
All day long
Like the moon
word
E - ter - nal pa - ra - dise
Sing in tune
Make your
hea - ven - ly joy
Cre - a - tions
bet
Race with sin
un - end - ing call
Close your eyes
Dreams will
Glo - ri - ous seed does grow
win
DS

Appendix 11

High in the hea - vens a - bove   Good-ness and glo - ry
shine   God's love is   true   truth does break through
Foun - tains of grace___ for you
Sweet breath of hea - ven - ly
joy   Wis - dom and won - ders a - bove
God's love to be   church sets us free
Faith___ helps___ you see
Ma ya ac cord helps you see

The author

Richard Byrne was born in Hull in 1956. He joined
the military where he was injured after seven years.
He attended Ulster University in Belfast and has
a BSC Hons degree in Community Development.
Richard was employed as a PCIH (Practitioner
Chartered Institute of Housing). He is an empa-
thetic, genuine and helpful person. His favourite
activities are golf and spending time with women.
He has travelled the world; has gone to Memphis
and Graceland, where he once shook hands with
Vesta Presley.
His published works are 1914 Dig the Dry Zone,
and 1916 Dig the Zone of Freedom available on the
internet. He is a single retired military veteran and
has no children.